Killer Chocolate Pie

A Pies and Pages Cozy Mystery

Book Two

BY

Carolyn Q. Hunter

Author's Note: On the next page, you'll find out how to access all of my books easily, as well as locate books by best-selling author, Summer Prescott. I'd love to hear your thoughts on my books, the storylines, and anything else that you'd like to comment on – reader feedback is very important to me. Please see the following page for my publisher's contact information. If you'd like to be on her list of "folks to contact" with updates, release and sales notifications, etc...just shoot her an email and let her know. Thanks for reading!

Also...

...if you're looking for more great reads, check out the Summer Prescott Publishing Book Catalog:

http://summerprescottbooks.com/book-catalog/ for some truly delicious stories.

Contact Info for Summer Prescott Publishing:

Twitter: @summerprescott1

Blog and Book Catalog: http://summerprescottbooks.com

Email: summer.prescott.cozies@gmail.com

And…look up The Summer Prescott Fan Page and Summer Prescott Publishing Page on Facebook – let's be friends! To sign up for our fun and exciting newsletter, which will give you opportunities to win prizes and swag, enter contests, and be the first to know about New Releases, click here:

https://forms.aweber.com/form/02/1682036602.htm

TABLE OF CONTENTS

KILLER CHOCOLATE PIE

A Pies and Pages Cozy Mystery Book Two

Prologue

"Are you serious, Dad?" Charleston Blinkerton's face took on a crimson shade of red while sweat collected along his dark hairline and his breathing quickened.

Standing in the cramped living room between his father's patchy leather recliner and the flat screen TV on the wall behind him, he fumed with silent anger. A Korean action movie played on the screen, something Daniel Blinkerton had stumbled upon while channel surfing.

"Son, do you mind moving out of the way?"

Charleston glanced back at the screen, his red expression wrinkling. "It's in Korean, Dad. You can't even understand it."

Leaning to one side, Daniel looked around his son to view the screen. An undercover cop was in the middle of a gun fight, shooting down anyone who got in his way. "It's an action movie, Charlie. What is there to understand?"

Refusing to be ignored, Charleston shuffled aside, blocking his father's view of the screen again.

"For heaven sake, boy. Move out of the way, will ya?"

"Don't call me that," he barked

"What?" Daniel asked, acting oblivious to his son's discomfort.

"Don't call me *boy*. I'm not a child."

"Then stop acting like one. You're twenty-four years old, for crying out loud," he snapped, leaning over to the other side of his chair and picking up his lite beer from the side table.

Baring his teeth like an angry dog, Charleston turned to the TV and punched the power button. In a blink of light, the movie disappeared into blackness.

"What the heck do you think you're doing?" the furious father exclaimed, standing up to turn the TV back on.

Charleston blocked his way, holding up a handful of shredded paper he'd found in the trash. "Look at this."

"Son, what is your problem?"

"This, dad. Did you do this?"

Daniel harrumphed, his lips squishing together like a fish. "It looks like a bunch of paper to me."

"It was my loan application, for college. Did you seriously shred it before I could submit it?"

The father glared at his son, finally willing to play along. "Of course, I did."

"Why? Why would you do that?"

"Charlie, remind me again what it was you were planning on studying at this college?"

"Jazz music," he screamed, the veins in his neck thrumming with each pulse.

"Jazz music," he sneered.

"Yes, you knew that. You knew that it's always been my dream to study music."

Stretching his arms out, he gripped his son's shoulders. "Charlie, we've discussed this. You don't have a talented bone in your body. You can't keep rhythm, you have no sense of time, and you always sing off-key. I refuse to help pay for a wasted education."

"It isn't a waste. Besides, you won't have to pay for it. That is the whole reason I was applying for student loans."

Daniel's mouth remained in a soured frown, like he'd just eaten a bad grape. He shook his head. "That's where you're wrong. I already know I'd end up paying for it in the end. You've never been able to hold down a job for more than a few months. You'd end up broke and unable to pay off that debt. And who would have to come in to save you?"

"That won't happen, Dad. Not this time."

"I'm sorry. No. I can't risk it, and I don't have the money to help."

Charleston's mouth twisted down into a frown. "You don't have the money? What about all those investments you've made throughout the years?"

"Most didn't pan out. You know that."

"But you're always giving Abigail tons of money to buy clothes and stuff. Maybe if you just stopped wasting money on her, you'd have a little to help me."

"Abigail is a girl, and girls need more attention."

"She's twenty-five and isn't a little girl. She doesn't need pampering," his voice cracked.

"Even if I had the extra money, I wouldn't help pay for your college. I refuse to let you throw money and years away getting a music degree you aren't even capable of using."

Shrugging off his father, he took a step back. "You're serious?"

"I'm dead serious, son. There is absolutely no way I'm allowing it."

"Mom would have supported me."

"Your mother isn't here anymore, remember? She left two years ago with no intentions of seeing us again. How is that for support?"

The tiniest tremble in the son's lip indicated a mixture of anger and sorrow. "You never believed in me. Ever!"

"I'm just being realistic," he said flatly.

His frown deepening, Charleston stomped off toward the front door, grabbing the black leather gun holster from the table.

"Where are you going, son?"

"The shooting range," he grunted, toting the rifle in the air before stepping out into the darkness of the late autumn eve.

Chapter 1

B ertha Hannah arrived at *Pies and Pages*, her combination pie shop and book store, around five in the morning. It was a chilly Saturday in early October. In a matter of weeks, the temperatures in Culver's Hood, Nebraska had dropped from warm, to cool, to cold. While it hadn't reached the frigid levels that winter would bring, Bert was still glad to get inside the warmth of her shop.

Her tan leather jacket acted as a great wind breaker, but didn't work quite so well against the chill in the early morning air. Closing the door behind herself, she walked behind the book counter and turned on the shop's lights.

An instant warmth filled the room as the hanging light fixtures—mimicking Victorian decorating styles—cast their soft yellow glow in between the wooden shelves and tables.

The rustle of dry leaves blowing around outside in the cold morning breeze were an added measure of comfort. Bert was a fan of all the seasons, but autumn and winter topped the charts for her. She loved being bundled up in front of the fire with a good book, or heating the house with the oven while baking one of her famous pies.

She could almost sense the holidays coming, which brought some extra cheer to the shorter days.

Removing her scarf, hand knitted from a soft burgundy wool, she walked under the brick archway into the pie shop and reading nook. Comfortable couches and chairs were accompanied by tables, an inviting setting where patrons could sit with a good book and enjoy a piece of scrumptious pie.

Speaking of pie, Bert thought as she looked about her cozy little shop, there was a ton of work to be done before she opened for the day. It had been nearly a week since the shop's grand opening, but the influx of customers had been steadily increasing. In fact, she'd even gained a few daily regulars already.

Today, however, she knew to expect a larger wave of people coming to her shop, asking for a slice of warm pie to ward off the cold, or seeking the latest mystery novel. It was the annual Autumn Walk, and all sorts of people would be in the downtown *Old Market* to view the changing leaves.

The pie shop was modeled after Victorian and Edwardian shops of a similar nature. A large glass display case with a solid oak base was available to display all the pies she would make for the day. Behind the case was a large wooden counter where she did most of the baking, right where the patrons could see her.

There was even a false metal door installed on the wall to give the illusion of a brick oven.

Moving behind the case, Bert hung her purse, jacket, and scarf on the antique coat rack and slipped on her red and black checkered apron. Stepping over to the fridge and freezer, built straight into the dark wood cabinetry, she retrieved the puff pastry dough from inside that she'd prepared the night before.

The rest of the morning was a blur of baking, the thought of the official Autumn Walk event beginning at ten o'clock looming on the horizon. The trees were all at their peak of reds and golds, giving the whole district a classic fall feeling. Farmers and vendors would be setting up booths all along the cobblestone streets, and shop owners would be doing sidewalk sales.

Bert was planning on putting out bins of used books and selling them for about a dollar a piece. She had so much back stock in old romance, mystery, and sci-fi softcovers that she felt she might just drown if she didn't clear out some of it soon. There were even boxes of old car, gun, and farming machinery manuals in the upstairs apartment which she had yet to decide what to do with.

She had her sights set on renovating and moving into the apartment, thus cutting down her twenty-minute commute to less than a few seconds. She even planned to put her cottage in uptown available for rent to make a little extra money. However, she needed to clear out the apartment first.

All of this would be easier if she'd just taken the time to hire one or two employees, but she hadn't gotten around to it yet. Therefore, she was on her own for the time being.

Most important of all, she needed to get a good selection of pies finished and inside the display case before opening hours. People would be hungry for a sweet brunch when ten o'clock rolled around.

Unfolding the puff pastry dough and laying it flat in a shallow pie dish, she trimmed the edges and slid it into the oven as it was still warming. It was going to be her specialty dish of the day, and she hoped it would bring in many customers from the Autumn Walk.

Her mouth was already watering.

Chapter 2

When opening time rolled around, the streets were filled with patrons milling about, all seeking to enjoy the colors of autumn, as well as the best deals on sale items. Bert had managed to roll out four metal bins full of used paperbacks in front of the shop's windows and already had interested customers looking over what she had in stock.

Having picked out a few interesting titles, she put up a single display shelf for the featured items. A few books by Ray Bradbury, Isaac Asimov, Agatha Christie, and Jane Austen graced the shelf—all authors that Bert favored.

She sat in a red lawn chair next to a small round table which contained free samples of her specialty pie of the day.

"Oh, Bert. This looks wonderful," Carla Young exclaimed as she approached the shop. Carla owned the *Christmas in July* shop that was situated just down the block and around the corner. It was a year-round Christmas store that sold ornaments, miniature houses, trinkets, trees, and more.

"Morning, Carla," Bert greeted her best friend. "What are you doing over here? I thought you'd be looking over your own shop."

"I left Jamie in charge for a minute while I came over to sneak a peek at what delightful things you had set up for the Autumn Walk."

Jamie was a local college student who worked for Carla during the evenings and weekends to make some extra cash.

"So, what's up for sample today?" Carla asked, clasping her hands eagerly and eyeing the treats on the silver platter with sparkling eyes.

"Here, try this one. It's my new favorite, I think." Bert lifted one of the paper serving cups with a small piece of pie in it. The fluffy crust was a pilot for what appeared to be chocolate and some kind of nut.

Carla took it without hesitation and tossed it in her mouth, munching away on the little piece of heaven. "Mmm. Oh my, Bert. What is this? It is unbelievable."

"I thought you might say that," she laughed, grabbing one of the samples herself and popping it into her mouth. She knew she should save them for customers, but couldn't help herself. After all, eating one wasn't going to make that much of a difference. "It's a tart, actually."

"Wow, sounds fancy."

"Not really. Just another word for pie. I baked it in a shallow pie tin."

"What's in it, besides chocolate?"

"Well, the crust is made of puff pastry."

"How do you make that?"

"I fold the flour dough around a block of butter and roll it out. I fold it again, and again, rolling it out every time. In the end, it creates

25

tiny layers of butter throughout the whole crust. When it bakes, it puffs up with little pockets of air between the layers."

"Wow. That sounds like a lot of work," Carla admitted, reaching out and taking another sample. Bert allowed it that one time. After all, she'd eaten a sample herself.

"Anyway, the filling is made of a thin layer of melted semi-sweet chocolate, drizzled with honey and salt. The final touch is slivered almonds along the top."

"Well, it's amazing," she admitted, reaching out for another sample.

"Hey, hey, hey," Bert playfully scolded.

"Sorry," Carla laughed. "I suppose I better just order a slice."

"Coming right up."

As Bert ran inside to grab a slice of the pie from the display case, a few other customers walked up and began to peruse the selection of books. One was an older gentleman with a beer branded ball cap on his head and large aviator sunglasses over his face. With him were two younger people, both appearing to be in their twenties. One was a man with messy dark hair, a slightly pointed nose, and glasses. The second was an attractive woman with brown hair that hung straight over her shoulders.

Stepping back outside and handing the slice of pie to Carla, Bert couldn't help but notice just how short the girl's little black skirt was, in spite of the chilly October air. A thin white long-sleeved shirt that left her shoulders completely uncovered also didn't seem to be very logical, and goosebumps were cropping up all along her skin.

"Would you folks like to try a sample of my chocolate-almond pie?" she offered, smiling as widely as possible.

"Sure, I'd love to," the girl exclaimed, reaching out and taking one.

The younger man simply stood in the background, glancing over the books with a furrowed brow. He appeared to be slightly agitated.

"Oh, Dad, this is so delicious," the girl exclaimed before she was even done chewing the bite.

"You like it, huh?" the man in the ball cap laughed.

The young man rolled his eyes.

"You have to try one," she squeaked, sounding like a pre-teen girl.

Bert found the young woman's behavior a little strange, but assumed there were many girls who acted like that nowadays.

"Don't mind if I do," the older gentleman responded, also taking one of the samples and popping it into his mouth.

"Good, huh?" the girl said.

"It is pretty tasty," he admitted. "Hey, son, come and give this stuff a try. Even *you* might like it."

Bert couldn't help but noticed a slight hint of condescension in the father's voice.

"No, thanks," the young man sneered.

The dad harrumphed quietly and turned back to face his daughter. "Do you want one, honey?"

The girl's face lit up like a child's on Christmas as she leaned on her father affectionately. "You mean it?"

"How much for one of those pies?" the man asked.

"Looks like things are picking up. I'll head back to the shop. Come over and see me if you get a chance," Carla whispered, heading off with her slice of pie in hand.

"Are you interested in a slice like that woman just had, or the full pie?"

"A full pie," the father said proudly, puffing out his chest as his daughter linked her arm in his.

"It's twenty-five dollars."

"For a pie? What's in it, gold?" the young man scoffed arrogantly.

Bert couldn't help but lean over and correct him on his entitled attitude. "Well, considering that I charge four dollars for a single slice, I'd say that is a good deal."

"In what reality?" he muttered, still audible to the group.

"The lady is right, you know, Charlie. To hand make a pie like this one probably takes some work, and I'm sure the ingredients aren't cheap."

"It's true. I only use the best," Bert responded.

"We'll take one full pie, thank you," the man declared proudly digging into his wallet and producing the exact change for the dish.

"Oh, thank you, Dad," the girl cried, embracing her father in a tight hug.

As Bert accepted the man's money and headed inside to grab one of the pies, she couldn't help but wonder if the girl really was as ditzy and airheaded as she seemed, or if it was part of an act to please her father.

Either way, she decided it was none of her business and pushed the thought aside.

Pulling out the pie, she carefully laid it inside one of the cardboard dessert boxes that made transporting the dish easier. As she was closing it, she could still hear the family's strained voices echoing through the open doorway.

"Seriously? Twenty-five dollars for a stupid pie, but not a cent for my college fund?"

"I thought we'd settled this last night, boy."

"Stop calling me that, dang it."

"When you've made your own money, you can spend it however you want. For now, I'm going to buy what I like, for whoever I like."

Bert glanced up and noticed the daughter batting her eyes at her brother—mocking him about her father's favoritism.

"Oh, and Abigail gets whatever she wants?"

"That's none of your business, is it, Charleston?"

"And I suppose if she were trying to invest in some stocks or the branch of a food chain or something, you'd spot her?" he snapped.

"I would do no such thing. You know that women aren't good with managing money."

Bert couldn't help but silently balk at this horrid statement. Still, she held her own feelings in reserve as she added the money to the till.

"And if *I* want to invest in something?"

"I wouldn't give you any money, either."

Bert didn't want to go out there during their mess of an argument, but didn't see any other choice. The sooner she gave them their pie, the sooner they would be on their way. She was sure the strained family was driving away other interested customers.

She knew she better get out there sooner than later and kindly shoo them along.

The young man's mouth hung open in shock. "What? Are you serious? You've spent your whole life doing business investing. Now you're telling me you wouldn't support me in that either?"

"Many of those projects failed. It's too risky nowadays, and you don't have a brain for business."

"But I don't have the talent for music, either? Is there a single thing I'm good for?"

"Here is your pie, sir," Bert announced, stepping out of the front door and interrupting the conversation.

"This whole thing is bogus," the son screamed, drawing the attention of passersby. "I swear, if you weren't my own father, I'd kill you." The next moment he was stomping off down the sidewalk and disappearing around the corner.

"Don't mind him," the father noted as he took the pie. "Thanks for this. We appreciate it. Don't we, darling?"

"Thanks, Dad," the daughter giggled.

Her silly, girlish behavior was starting to get on Bert's nerves. What self-respecting woman would allow themselves to appear like that in public?

"See anything else you want?" he asked, clearly looking to spoil her more.

Bert was forced to work hard not to drop her smile. The father's apparent favoritism between the two adult children was sickening. Of course, it didn't help that the daughter just ate it up.

Abigail hummed as she scanned over the book bin in front of her. "I'd also like to buy this," she pointed at an old, yet very advanced, technical manual about various types of hand guns and rifles.

"Oh, you don't want that. Guns are a man's sport."

Abigail scoffed, making a clicking sound in the back of her throat. "But you taught Charlie to shoot when he was only eight," she argued, the overly sweet tone of voice dropping slightly for the first time.

Bert was beginning to suspect more and more that the sweetness was just a false cover.

"That's because he is a boy, dear. It was father, son time when I took him out to the shooting range." He tapped the cover of the technical manual. "Besides, this book would be way above your head."

"No, it wouldn't," she snapped, stomping her foot like a child.

He reached down and picked up a copy of *Pride and Prejudice*. "How about this instead? I think a lot of women your age like it."

"No, thank you, Dad," she grumbled.

"Are you sure? I know you ladies love your romances."

"No, Dad. Forget it," she screamed, even louder than her brother had. Letting go of his arm, she stomped off down the street.

The father shrugged his shoulder at Bert. "I guess she can be a little spoiled sometimes." He laughed it off.

"I'm sure she isn't," Bert lied, putting on a good face for the customer. In another other situation, she would have called him out, gave him a piece of her mind. However, just as her late husband Howie had taught her, this was business. It was her first truly difficult encounter with a patron, but she tried to not let it get to her.

He set the copy of *Pride and Prejudice* down on the table next to Bert's cashbox. "How much for the book? I'm sure she would want to read it."

CAROLYN Q. HUNTER

Chapter 3

The platter of chocolate-almond tart samples quickly vanished in a matter of a few minutes, and Bert hustled back inside to prepare another round of them. She hadn't expected to sell a whole pie so early in the day and was worried she might run out of the specialty dish before too long.

If it came down to it, she'd have to skip her lunch break to bake more of the pies for the afternoon patrons of the Autumn Walk.

Pulling out the tart she had cut Carla's piece from, she began slicing up the tiny bite sized portions that would entice customers to come in and buy books and pie. Carefully arranging them in the paper cups on the platter so they'd look pretty, she headed back toward the front door.

She froze in place upon seeing Abigail, the strange girl from just moments before, bent over the book bin.

"Not again," Bert whispered. She'd thought she was done dealing with that family of troublesome customers already. Why was the daughter back so soon?

Bert only had one guess.

Taking a deep breath, she stepped outside and set the sample tray down on the table. "Hello. Back again?" She plastered a big smile on her face, hoping she could help the girl and get her on her way quickly.

"Hey, I was wondering if you still had that book, the one about rifles," she asked in a normal, somewhat monotone voice. The girlish lilt and high-pitched squeak she'd had before was now vanished into a seemingly more mature, albeit still entitled, young woman.

From one moment to the next, this girl seemed to have such varied moods and behaviors.

"Of course," Bert answered her without comment on the girl's odd personality. Digging into the bin, she presented the book. "Is this the one you were looking for?"

"That's the one. How much?" she asked.

"Two dollars."

"Sold," Abigail declared, digging into her purse.

Bert paused thinking of the conversation from earlier and taking the opportunity to offer the girl an even better deal. "You know, this book is fairly advanced. It's for people who've been shooting or hunting for a number of years."

Abigail's straight face wrinkled into a scowl, making her look older than she actually was. "So, what?"

"I'm just saying, if it's true that you're new to the sport of range shooting, I'd like to recommend something else."

"Excuse me?"

Bert dug through the book bin and retrieved a beginner's manual she had remembered being in there. "Now, this book is an excellent starting point for anyone considering getting into hobby shooting. It's actually what I read back when my husband taught me the sport. It's old, but very reliable."

Abigail's nose crinkled up and her cheeks flushed red. "Are you serious, right now?"

Bert was surprised by the girl's sudden flash of anger. It was as if she could flip a switch and change from one emotion to the next without so much as a moment's warning in between. She tried to ignore it, continuing with her offer. "I'm willing to sell it to you for fifty-cents. My way of saying thanks for your patronage."

"I'm not interested in your stupid children's book," she barked, the flush spreading from her cheeks and into the rest of her face.

"I was just trying to offer you something more at your level."

"You're just like my dad," she spit through gritted teeth.

"Whatever do you mean?" Bert asked, taken aback by the woman's behavior.

"I *mean* that you're old, condescending, and stupid."

Bert was forced into complete and utter silence by the girl's words, her mouth hanging open in shock. Never had anyone spoken to her in such a degrading manner, especially not a younger person.

"I don't want your dumb suggestions or opinions. You don't know me, and you don't know my dad. I want that book," she yelled, pointing at the advanced manual. The childish attitude from earlier was resurfacing ten-fold. A nearby family with children were all gawking at the scene.

Bert, without another thought, picked up the book in question and set it behind the bin. "I'm sorry. That item is no longer for sale."

"What?" the girl screeched.

"I'm telling you. The book isn't up for sale. You can take your business elsewhere."

"You can't do that. I'm a paying customer, you old hag."

Bert felt a sudden rush of blood to her head, making her slightly dizzy. It didn't stop the overflowing barrage of words that came next. "Look here, young lady. You've done nothing but act rude and demanding today as you've been at my shop. You've called me names when I've done nothing but try to help you and give you options."

"I don't want your stupid options."

"Clearly not, but until you can learn to behave like a woman your age, you are not welcome here. Now, I'm going to ask you to leave one more time before I am forced to call *Old Market* security to escort you out."

Abagail leaned over the bin, her eyes flashing with a fiery spark. "Forget you, lady. Who cares? Keep your stupid old book." With that, she was stomping off down the street again.

Bert couldn't help but wonder exactly what was wrong with that girl.

CAROLYN Q. HUNTER

Chapter 4

The rest of the morning went by in a blur of pie samples and book sales. A lot more people came by the shop and purchased either slices of pie, or even whole pies. She'd even had to restock the book bins twice with merchandise from the store rooms and apartment because they were starting to look sparse. The Autumn Walk was helping Bert make a killing that day.

If she continued to do business like this every weekend, she'd pay off her costs for the renovations in no time.

Around two, things had begun to slow down a little. In the lull, Bert thought it might be a good time to take a quick break and head over to *Christmas in July* to see how Carla was doing with her sidewalk sales.

Bringing the sample tray inside, Bert locked up the shop and headed one block down and around the corner to Carla's place. She simply left the book bins outside, deciding she was only going to be gone a minute and the books would be okay.

Turning the corner, Bert was shocked to see an elaborate Christmas themed display that put her own shop to shame. The sidewalk was decorated like a quaint living room. A portable, electric fireplace which put off heat was up against the building, decorated with a miniature village on top (each piece of the village was marked with a price). A red and white rug lay on the ground with a plush chair and a coffee table on it. There was even a Christmas tree with ornaments for sale against one of the windows. Carla sat in the chair, handing out candy canes to all the children.

"Wow, you really went all out," Bert proclaimed upon approaching her friend.

"Oh, it's nothing I haven't done every year." She waved a dismissive hand at the compliment. "I always like to kick off the holiday shopping season with a bang."

"I guess so," Bart laughed.

"Who is watching your shop?"

"No one," she admitted, giving a timid shrug.

"No one?"

"Naw, I figured I'd only be gone for a second, so it wouldn't matter."

"Well, I would get back as soon as possible. I don't trust people."

Bert furrowed her brow, thinking of Abigail from earlier. What would stop the angry girl from coming back and stealing books or vandalizing the shop? She seemed like the kind of person with just a few screws loose who would do it. "Did something happen over here?" she asked, wondering if the crazy family had caused distress elsewhere.

"You just missed all the craziness."

"What do you mean?"

"Well, Reba who runs the *Candy Emporium* next door got in a shouting match with some guy in a beer cap."

Bert's eyes widened suspiciously. "The same guy who was over at my place earlier?"

"Yeah, I think that's the one."

"What the heck were they arguing about?"

Carla shrugged. "I can't say for sure. Reba was screaming about pompous men or something like that."

Bert's wonder instantly disappeared. "Oh, I see."

"What is it?" her friend pressed, recognizing the look on her face.

"Oh, he just said a few things I didn't agree with earlier, like women couldn't really run a business. Honestly, that son and daughter of his weren't much better."

"How can anyone think that in this day and age, you know? After all, you, me, and Reba all run our businesses nearly on our own."

"It's true, but some people are just old-fashioned I guess."

"Outdated is more like it."

Bert chuckled. "I'm sure you and I are not exactly the hippest people on the block."

"Yes, even you saying the word *hippest* shows that," Carla teased.

"Face it. We're old ladies."

"Yeah, but we aren't so behind the times that we think women should be at home in the kitchen," Carla noted, returning to the subject at hand.

"Did he say that?" Bert wouldn't be surprised if he had.

"I think so. He mentioned how it was so good of Reba to help her husband run the business, even when she had 'duties' at home."

"Wow," Bert mouthed wondrously.

"Anyway, Reba went off on him. You know how short a temper she has. She said she was the business owner, didn't have a husband, and never intended to have one."

Bert knew that Rebecca Stallion—whom everyone called Reba for short—had a very short fuse. She was known to speak her mind on more than one occasion. In some ways, Bert was surprised she didn't drive off more customers. However, Bert knew she wasn't one to judge, thanks to the fact that she herself had lost her temper that day at the young woman named Abigail.

Still, she had a deep respect for Reba. She was strong willed and knew what she wanted in life.

"What happened after that?" Bert asked.

"He told her she had no right to talk to him like that. He, as a man, deserved more respect."

"Holy smokes. I'm glad I didn't say anything when he was shooting his mouth off at my place."

"No kidding. Anyway, the *Old Market* security guys had to come over and ask him to leave."

"Were either of his kids with him?" Bert wondered out loud, thinking it would only add insult to injury.

"Which ones?" Carla asked.

"He had two twenty-something kids with him."

"Oh, yes. I remember them. No, I didn't see either of them. He was on his own."

Bert hummed thoughtfully. "Yep. They both huffed off earlier. I'm not surprised."

"Anyway, that's the gossip for today. You better get back to your shop before someone steals all your books."

Bert gave a playful salute. "I'm on my way." After her own encounter with Abigail, and hearing the craziness that had happened at the *Candy Emporium*, she was feeling anxious that she'd left her books unattended.

Hustling back around the corner, Bert was surprised when a loud pop noise rang out through the air. Jumping and letting out a quiet yelp, she turned curiously in a circle, trying to see exactly where the sound had come from.

A squeak drew her attention across the street.

There was a clown standing outside the *FunWorld* toy and game shop where the wooden sign was swinging back and forth—squeaking quietly. He was apologizing to a little kid while disposing of the limp remains of a balloon in one of his gloved hands. The fragmented rubber hit the side of the miniature trashcan on his cart, but fell onto the sidewalk where he didn't notice it. In the next moment, he was filling another balloon to make a replacement.

"Woo," Bert gasped, putting a hand over her heart. That had given her quite the start. For a second, she'd thought it was a gunshot it was so loud.

The sign continued to swing for a second, and then finally stopped. Bert found it odd since she hadn't felt a gust of wind. She guessed the popping balloon could have caused it to move.

Walking back down the block, her shop came into view.

Despite her earlier thoughts that all the books would be okay, she eagerly glanced to see if someone had made off with all her books.

It was a silly thought, instilled in her brain by her friend, but she had been concerned, nonetheless.

Much to her delight, all the bins appeared to be completely full still, as did the main display.

There was, however, one item out of place.

"Oh, no," Bert whispered. A man in a familiar ball cap and sunglasses sat in her lawn chair. What the heck did he think he was doing?

Hoping she wouldn't have any trouble convincing him to move, she jogged the rest of the way to her shop.

"Excuse me, sir, but do you mind moving?" she asked in as a polite a voice as she could muster. If he gave her any flack, she wouldn't hesitate to call security.

The man didn't respond at all, but simply sat with a blank look on his face.

"Sir?" she asked, wondering if he was asleep. Touching him on the shoulder, he toppled over onto the sidewalk his glasses toppling from his face and cracking on the pavement. The boxed chocolate-almond tart in his lap went spilling everywhere on the sidewalk.

Bert let out a surprised shriek upon seeing the bloody gunshot wound in his chest.

Chapter 5

In less than five minutes, the street in front of *Pies and Pages* was filled with emergency vehicles. Two police cars, an ambulance, and even a firetruck all arrived, their lights flashing for all the patrons of the Autumn Walk to see. Crime scene tape cordoned off the entire entryway to the shop, leaving the pies inside to simply sit uneaten.

Detective Harold Mannor, a stout man in his late sixties, was rushing back and forth, giving orders, asking questions, and making ample use of any daylight he had left

Meanwhile, Bert stood off to the side watching all the chaos happen. The Detective, who had become acquainted with Bert recently, didn't even acknowledge she was there. She figured he would want to question her eventually, so she was sticking nearby.

She could hardly believe it. A man had been murdered right out front of her pie shop and bookstore—shot in the middle of a downtown fair with not a single person noticing.

How was that possible? Was there just so much noise, so much going on, that the murder went unnoticed until Bert stumbled upon the body? Or, had the body been moved to the street and left in the chair?

If the latter were the case, how come no one noticed a suspicious person dragging a body over and plopping it down in a chair.

The victim didn't look like he was lightweight in any sense of the word. He was tall, with a strong build and a beer belly. You'd have to be fairly strong to move a man of that size.

Bert shook her head. It didn't make any sense.

At that same moment, a large black catering van from a local coffee chain pulled up. The name *Koffee Hous* was written on the side in bright red lettering and two girls dressed in matching black uniforms climbed out. Quickly retrieving multiple caddies full of coffee, the girls walked up to the crime scene tape and—without stepping into the area—started handing out the drinks.

Bert thought it was an odd display, but figured even the police needed their boost occasionally, especially during a homicide investigation.

"Can you believe the nerve of that company?" came a huff from behind Bert.

Turning around, she was surprised to see Reba standing there with a stern line for a mouth and her arms folded. "Reba, how are you doing?" Bert asked, aware that the woman didn't much care for her, but trying to be civil anyway.

"That darn coffee chain shouldn't be allowed to sell their drinks here. It's against the historic code."

Bert shook her head. "I'm sorry. I must be confused."

Reba rolled her eyes. "Them, those coffee people. The *Old Market* has a strict code that no chain businesses are allowed to sell their product here."

Bert glanced back at the two girls handing out the coffees. "Well, I'm sure that only applies to the actual store locations in the market, right? I mean, if someone orders a drink delivery and asks them to drop it off here, they should be able to do that, right?"

"No, it shouldn't be allowed," she barked.

"Oh, I see."

"They're stealing customers away from honest small businesses like ours."

Bert thought about this complaint for a second and then returned with another comment. "Wait, do you sell coffee at your candy shop?"

Reba gaped at Bert with an open mouth. "Of course not."

"Is there even a coffee shop in the *Old Market*?"

"That is beside the point," she exclaimed. "I've met the district manager of that local chain. He's a ruthless, hardened, rude man. If it were up to him, we'd all be out of business and replaced with *Koffee Hous* franchises."

Bert rolled her eyes at Reba's over-exaggerating. "If there isn't an official coffee shop here, who are they stealing coffee from? I mean, I admit I sell plain coffee, or coffee with cream, in the pie shop— but I don't have any kind of gourmet flavors or anything."

Reba folded her arms. "I should have known you'd be on their side. Stealing business from me, and now you're in cahoots with a company like *Koffee Hous*."

"I have no idea what you're talking about," Bert admitted, giving a sheepish shrug. Reba really knew how to blow things out of proportion.

"Them and their disgusting pumpkin spice flavored drinks," she sneered quietly, not addressing Bert's defense.

She paused, tapping her foot. "Well, I happen to enjoy pumpkin spiced coffee."

Reba wrinkled her nose in disgust. "I'm not surprised."

Bert held her tongue, realizing now was not the time for debate over chain brand coffee shops versus local coffee shops. She was honestly surprised that *Koffee Hous* was the one thing Reba was focusing on when there had just been a murder in the *Old Market*.

"Why am I getting the feeling of dejavu?" a man said from behind the caution tape.

Turning away from Reba, Bert spotted Detective Mannor heading her way. "Detective. I'm glad you're the one assigned to this case," she admitted. It was the truth. Back in August, the previous owner of the book shop had been murdered and Detective Mannor had helped in catching the culprit.

"Are you now?" he asked, not sounding convinced.

Bert titled her head, her eyelids drooping slightly. "Truly, Detective. A familiar face at a time like this is always welcome, even if it's only yours." She didn't mean for her last comment to sound rude, but she realized it came off that way.

Mannor took the tone of the comment and ran with it. "I do find it a little odd that two murders happened at your shop now, each within a few months of one another."

"I knew she was bad news," Reba shot in without any qualms.

The detective raised an irritated eyebrow at the strange woman's intrusion. "And you are?"

Placing her hand on her chest, Reba gasped. "Detective, I'm surprised at you. You don't remember me?"

"Haven't the foggiest, ma'am," he admitted without a hint of care or remorse.

"I'm Rebecca Stallion, owner of the *Candy Emporium* around the corner."

"I see," he grunted, clearly not wanting any unnecessary people hanging around the crime scene. "And, did you happen to *see* the murder occur, or are you just an interested spectator?"

"Believe me, Detective. I would not be over here unless I absolutely had to be. Especially with the trash that seems to be hanging around." She motioned to the *Koffee Hous* van.

"Trash?" Bert groaned.

"Money grubbing companies like that one, aren't allowed to sell here on the *Old Market* property."

Mannor nodded humorously, holding back a smirk of enjoyment about what he was about to say next. "Well, it's a good thing they aren't selling anything."

"I can see them handing out coffee as we speak," she blurted out, pointing at the two girls who had just finished emptying the caddies.

"Oh, you see, that's because whenever the police in this city have a large investigation like a murder, *Koffee Hous* tries to provide free drinks if they can." He finally let the smirk through, causing Bert to chuckle under her breath. She had no idea that the detective had such a wicked humor about him. Of course, to face murder and other violent crime on a regular basis, she figured you just had to have a sense of humor.

Meanwhile, Reba was flabbergasted. "W-Well. They still shouldn't be advertising here," she attempted to argue, losing steam.

"Why not? I'm a fan of the pumpkin spice, myself," he admitted, sipping his coffee and make a satisfied noise.

"F-fine. I see how it is. I was going to share what I saw today, but now maybe I won't," she threatened uselessly, turning to leave.

Bert was honestly appalled at her complete lack of regard for an official police investigation. If Reba truly had some piece of evidence to add to the case, she should present it without any precursor.

"Hold on," he ordered, his serious tone coming back ten-fold.

"Yes?" she asked.

"You are aware that it is a crime to withhold any evidence, any at all, about a murder case such as this one?"

Reba bit her lower lip, suddenly turning red. "Of course, I knew that," she lied.

Bert wondered how often Reba just lost her head like that, saying whatever angry thing popped into her head.

"Well?" he pressed, trying to assess the situation and see if the information she claimed to have was worth even hearing.

Reba stuttered slightly, but finally got started in her statement. "I-I overheard that the victim was an older man wearing a beer hat and aviators?"

"That would be an accurate description. Did you see the victim earlier today?"

"You said he was found sitting in a lawn chair in front of this shop?"

"That's where I found him, yes," Bert chimed in.

"Mrs. Hannah, please let me handle this," the detective said, holding up a hand to silence her.

"Sorry," she apologized.

"Well, he came over to my shop earlier and was arguing with me," Reba admitted.

Bert wasn't sure admitting you'd had it out with a murder victim right before they bit the dust was the best choice of action, but it wasn't her place to judge. After all, the argument would probably come out later, anyway.

"Can you tell me what the argument was about?" he asked, setting his coffee down on the hood of the nearby police cruiser and pulling out a pad and pen. Clearly, he had decided whatever she had to report was important.

"Politics mostly. Feminism."

"I see. You two disagreed on this topic?"

"Ha. I'd say we were night and day. He got so riled up that the security guard had to escort him off the premises."

The detective scribbled something down, likely a note to check the story with the guard on duty. "What happened after that?"

"Well, I wanted to make sure that he had really left the *Old Market*. I didn't want him coming back around, you know? Who knows what a crazy man like that might do for revenge."

Bert couldn't help but roll her eyes at this comment.

The detective shot her a scolding look before returning to his line of questioning. "Now. Did you see him again?"

"I did. I watched him come back up Jefferson Street. He stopped outside the book shop, looked around expectantly, checked his phone, and sat down in the lawn chair."

Bert considered what reason the man might have for returning to the pie shop. She figured that maybe he was backtracking to find his son and daughter. It would explain him checking his phone, seeing if one of his kids had sent a text. Maybe they had driven together to the Autumn Walk.

"Now, just to clarify, the victim was *alive* when he sat down?"

"That's right."

"And did you see anyone at all come up to him? Any sign of someone recognizing the victim?"

She shrugged. "I have no idea. After he sat down, I left to find the security guard again to have the man removed."

"Anything else I should know about, ma'am?"

Reba twisted her face up as she thought. "I don't think so."

Mannor thought for a moment before posing his next question. "Own any guns, ma'am?"

"Of course, I do. Who wouldn't in this day and age? I have a right to protect myself and my property."

"I see. Where do you store these weapons?"

"I have a cabinet in my basement at home, but also have my concealed carry if you catch my drift."

Mannor's furrowed brow indicated he clearly understood. "And you're adept at handling these firearms?"

"You're darn right, I am. I just told you I had my carry license, didn't I? What's the point of having them if I don't even know how to turn off the safety? I make sure to practice at least once a month out at my brother's ranch house."

Bert was surprised. She would have never pegged Reba as a hobby shooter.

The detective tapped his pen on the pad. "I see."

Reba raised a suspicious eyebrow. "Now, just a minute. What are you getting at here?"

"Thank you for your time," he replied, not answering her question. Thankfully, Reba let it slide. "I'm going to have one of my officer's take down your information." He waved over a younger man.

"My information? What for? I'm not a suspect, am I?"

"It's preliminary measure, I assure you, just in case we need any more information."

She paused, still unsure about handing out her info. The officer, however, was already getting a form ready. "Oh, very well," she sighed, moving off to the side with the cop.

With her out of earshot, Detective Manor looked directly at Bert.

"Mrs. Hannah, I think you and I should have a private chat, now."

Waving a finger, he instructed her to follow him into the shop.

Chapter 6

The scent of pumpkin spice coming off the detective's coffee was strong. Bert started to crave a drink herself, and made a mental note to stop by *Koffee Hous* later. She took a seat at one of the small side tables in the pie shop.

"Don't touch anything while you're in here, got it? I realize this is your place of business, but until I reopen the crime scene to the public, you need to keep your hands to yourself."

"I wouldn't dream of it," she admitted, folding her arms to show her compliance. She was honestly surprised he was conducting this interview inside the shop, but guessed he must be tired and wanting a place to sit for a moment.

"Good."

"Now why do I get interviewed in here, but Reba gets to give her statement on the street?"

The detective looked less than amused. "Number one, you're the one who found the body—or so you say," he speculated.

"I say?" she protested.

He glossed over her small outburst. "Number two, you were smart enough not to barge in with your two cents worth while I was questioning the other witness outside. I can't trust someone like Ms. Stallion to do the same."

Bert nodded. "I understand."

"Good."

There was a moment's pause as Detective Mannor flipped through a few notes he had already taken about the crime scene.

"Did you get the apple pie I sent you?" she asked, breaking the silence.

Pausing, he looked up begrudgingly. "Are you trying to butter me up, Mrs. Hannah?"

"You can call me, Bert, you know? And, no. I'm not trying to butter you up—just offering a favor in return for a favor. After all, you *did* pay for my pizza a few weeks ago."

He flipped his notebook momentarily closed. "That was simply a thank you for your assistance in the murder case. The information you gave helped immensely."

"Of course. I just wanted to return the favor. That's why I dropped the pie on your doorstep."

The detective pushed his lips together, breathing out through his nose.

"Did you like it?" she pressed.

"Yes, it was one of the best pies I've ever eaten," he admitted in a muted voice, like it was impossible for him to admit he enjoyed something.

"Great, I'm glad to hear it."

"Great," he muttered, clearly wanting to get a move on.

"Hey, I still have some great pies sitting in the warmer. Do you want a piece?"

"No, thank you. Remember what I said about not touching anything?"

"Yes, sorry." She put up both hands defensively, showing she was being compliant. "I guess I just thought that, since the shop door was locked during the murder, maybe it was okay if we had the pies that I was keeping back here. If they don't get eaten, they go to waste at the end of the day."

The detective rubbed his lips together, licking them hungrily. Bert wondered if he'd had anything to really eat that day.

Finally, he shook his head. "No, just in case, I can't let you do that."

"He wasn't poisoned, you know," she said.

Flipping his notepad back open, he poised his pen. "Can we move forward with this interview now?"

"Of course, I'm sorry."

"Now, first things first. You claim you found the murder victim?"

"That's correct. He was sitting in my lawn chair out front."

"And he was dead?"

"Well, I didn't realize it at first. I thought he had just taken a seat to wait for his son and daughter and fallen asleep."

The detective took a note, and Bert could see it said *son and daughter.*

"When did you realize he was dead?"

"Well, I went to shake him awake, and he fell out of the chair onto the concrete. I saw the gunshot wound, and I knew he was dead."

"How did you know it was a gunshot wound?" he asked, tapping his pen on the top of his pad.

"When my husband was alive, he used to take me on his hunting trips in the Rocky Mountains. I've seen what it looks like when you snipe a rabbit or a deer. The wound looked like that."

"You know a lot about guns?"

"Not really. I usually just used a twenty-two rifle. It's my favorite gun. I don't know much about other guns."

The detective wrote down the number twenty-two. "Anything else stick out to you about the moment you found the body?"

"Yes, actually. He was still carrying the pie he bought from me earlier. A chocolate-almond tart. The box was in his lap. When he fell, the pie went everywhere. It was a real waste, honestly."

The detective was nodding, silently adding his agreement and licking his lips again.

"Are you sure you don't want a piece of pie?"

"And where were you before that point?" he asked, ignoring her question and sipping his coffee.

"I had locked up for just a minute so I could run over to the *Christmas in July* shop and see my friend's sidewalk display."

"And that friend is?"

"Carla Young is her name."

He scribbled it down.

"What time did you leave?"

"Just after two in the afternoon."

"And about what time did you head back?"

"Three to five minutes later. I wasn't gone that long."

"Enough time for the victim to take a seat and get shot."

"Seems like a very close call, you know?"

"Well, considering Ms. Stallion didn't see the murder occur, it's a very limited amount of time." He picked up the coffee again and drank from it. "Did you notice anything strange on your way back to the shop? Anyone walking away from the shop, or anyone dressed suspiciously?" He was grasping for anything at this point that might point to a description of the killer.

"I didn't see anyone, but I heard a pop that I thought was a gunshot at first. It turned out just to be a balloon."

"A balloon?"

"The toy store had a clown giving out free balloons."

He made a note to talk to the toy shop owner. "And you didn't see anyone?" he reiterated.

"Not that I can remember. I only remember being surprised that the man was in my chair."

The detective pursed his lips, let out a long breath, and closed his notepad. "Okay. I think that will be all for the moment. I already have your information on file if I need to talk to you again."

"I'll be available."

"I assume you have mine."

"Right. From the last case."

"If you think of anything else. Give me a call."

"I will," she smiled, standing up and shaking his hand.

Chapter 7

"I still can't believe it happened," Carla admitted, setting a mug of hot chocolate in front of Bert.

"Thanks," she said, taking a sip. The dim glow of Christmas lights illuminated the break room at Carla's shop. After finishing her interview with Detective Mannor, Bert had headed over to see her friend.

Carla took a seat opposite Bert, cradling her own cup of steaming hot chocolate in her hands. "Two, Bert."

"Two what?"

"You've seen two dead bodies now, murder victims." With shaky hands, she drank from her mug. "I just can't imagine how you must be feeling."

Bert had to admit, as shocking as finding the dead man on her own shop front had been, she didn't feel the least bit shaken up about it now. In fact, Carla seemed more upset by the events than she was. Bert shrugged. "I've always been a fairly tough lady."

"I think I would have fainted either time," Carla whispered. "First a stabbing in your own shop, and now a shooting."

"I was shocked when I first found him. I mean, you don't just go about your day expecting to see a body with a bullet hole in its chest."

"I'd think not."

"But, I think about the Detective, or even the EMTs who arrived on the scene. They all deal with serious accidents and death on a daily basis. I suppose after a while you learn better coping mechanisms." She lifted her cup, drinking in the richness of the cream and chocolate together. "I guess I'm just learning quickly to push those things from my mind. If I didn't, I might end up an emotional wreck."

"I guess so." Carla reached over and grabbed her friend by the hand. "I've always admired your go-get-em attitude. Nothing seems to faze you."

"Believe me, it does. I'm just doing a good job keeping things under wraps."

Both women went silent for a moment as they sipped their drinks.

"At least, this time, it wasn't someone we both knew and were friends with," Carla admitted, referring to the death of the previous bookshop's owner.

"It's still shocking. His name was Daniel Blinkerton, according to the police, and he has two kids."

"Those twenty-somethings?"

"Yep. A son and daughter. I'm not sure if the detective managed to track them down yet and give them the bad news."

Carla chewed her lower lip. "Do you think it was one of them? You mentioned that they were the angry sort."

"Who knows? The son seemed miffed with his father. They had an argument about money and he stormed off. The daughter, too, seemed irritable. She was sort of full of herself, you know."

"They always are, aren't they?"

"Well, with the way her father was treating her, buying her things left and right, it was no surprise. Still, the way she flipped from one mood to another."

"So, you think it was the father's fault?"

"I'd say so. Anyway, when the father refused to buy his daughter a book on guns, she stomped off."

Carla's mouth dropped open. "A book on guns? You don't think?"

Bert waved her hand dismissively. "Naw. The girl seemed to be a few crayons short of a full box, sort of a ditz. I'm not so sure she'd know how to even hold a gun properly. It sounded like shooting guns was something her father refused to let her do. He said it was a man's sport."

"Wow. I guess it's no surprise he and Reba got into a fight." Carla stood up and deposited her empty mug in the sink.

"The detective seemed awfully interested in hearing about Reba's fight with him."

Turning around, Carla leaned on the sink. "You don't think she had anything to do with this, do you?"

Bert finished off her own drink and stood up. "I doubt it. Reba might be hot tempered and high strung, but can you really imagine her killing someone?"

"I guess not."

Bert headed over and put her cup in the sink as well. "Thanks for the drink, Carla. It really hit the spot after everything that happened today."

"Do you think you'll be able to open up tomorrow?"

"Most likely. I doubt that Detective Mannor will keep the building sealed off for too long."

Carla was shaking her head, her eyes wide and staring off into space. "It happened right in the middle of the Autumn Walk, and no one noticed. How did no one notice?"

Bert tilted her head to one side and sighed, leaning against the counter with her friend. "I didn't see anyone near the body when I was walking up, but that doesn't mean they weren't there. They had to have been. Especially, since Reba saw the victim sit down in the chair."

"Do you think Reba was telling the truth about seeing him?"

"I don't see why not. What possible reason would she have for lying?"

"You're probably right. Do you think it was premeditated? I mean, how else could someone have committed a murder in the short amount of time you were at my shop?"

Bert thought this over, realizing she was right. "It does seem like the only possible way, doesn't it?"

"I still don't understand how no one saw the killer."

"Or heard a gunshot?" Bert added, still confused about this little detail herself.

"Maybe they used a silencer?" Carla offered.

Bert shook her head. "No, silencers don't work the same way as the movies. There is still a pop noise."

"Like that balloon," Carla said.

Suddenly, a lightbulb turned on in Bert's mind. "Popped. That's exactly it! I have an idea."

Chapter 8

"What? What is it?" Carla begged for an answer as Bert was pulling on her jacket.

"It's already getting dark out, so I'm not sure if I'll be able to find anything." Zipping up, she threw the scarf around her neck.

"Find what?"

"I have to have a look."

"A look for what?" Carla asked again, grabbing her own jacket off the rack and following Bert as she headed down the steps from the breakroom and into the shop. "Jamie, watch the shop, please."

"Got it," the young shop-keep gave a thumbs up as the two older women bustled out the door.

The early evening chill was already setting in, creating goose pimples on the back of Bert's neck. Pulling her scarf tighter, she led the way down the sidewalk and around the corner—the same path she always took to get back to her shop. In the distance, the blinking lights of the two police cars remained on the site.

Bert guessed the body had officially been taken to the city morgue, probably for an autopsy.

Walking about halfway down the block, she stopped in her tracks.

"Oof," Carla exclaimed, nearly running into her friend.

"Sorry. I didn't mean to stop so suddenly."

"Bert, what in heaven's name are we doing? What are we looking for?"

She motioned with a nod of her head toward the dark toy shop across the street. It appeared that they had closed early after the murder had occurred.

Only the yellow illumination from the old gas street lamp—updated to use electric bulbs—granted any light to the scene.

Festive pumpkin, witch, and black bat paper cutouts adorned the windows. A selection of stuffed animals, dolls, and action figures stared out from behind the darkened glass, the outside lamps catching the plastic of their eyes. The large oak tree growing out of the sidewalk grate in front of the store let down a rain of leaves, shrouding the place in a frame of moving shadows.

A sinister aura hung in the air, sending chills up and down Bert's spine. Brushing off the uncomfortable sensation, she stepped out into the cobblestone street.

"Come on," she whispered, waving for Carla to follow.

"Seriously? What are we doing?"

"Do you want to come or not?"

There was a beat of hesitation on Carla's part, but she eventually groaned. Stepping off the sidewalk, she couldn't help but shiver. "It's spooky."

"The toy shop?"

"Yeah. Look at all those eyes watching us." She pointed at the unblinking dolls.

"They're just toys, Carla."

"I know that, but it's still creepy," she admitted as they reached the sidewalk on the other side.

Bert began scanning the ground.

"What the heck are you looking for?" Carla insisted on knowing.

"I heard a balloon pop earlier."

"Yeah, the clown was handing them out and popped one. You told me that because it scared you."

"And it sounded like a muffled gunshot."

Suddenly, Carla's eyes widened. "You mean, you think the killer shot him from way over here?"

"Of course, don't you see? How else would they go undiscovered? They probably had the gun concealed, maybe in a jacket or something to quiet the sound, and used the sound of a balloon popping to hide any residual noise. Even with a silencer *and* a jacket or blanket or something, the gun would still be heard."

Carla's jaw dropped. "That's horrible. They shot the balloon right out of the clown's hand?"

"They'd have to be a phenomenal shot, someone who's been practicing for years, but I think it's possible."

"You think the balloon is still out here?"

"I saw it fall out of the trash, so I'm hoping it is." Bert crouched down near the sidewalk to have a look.

"They probably swept up after the Autumn Walk ended."

"Maybe, but if I can find the remnants of that balloon, Detective Mannor can run some tests on it. Maybe there is gunpowder residue or something."

Carla folded her arms. "You've been watching too many crime shows."

"Got it!" Bert exclaimed loudly. Standing up, she presented the pink remains of what had once been a balloon.

"Detective Mannor isn't going to be able to do anything with that," Carla said. "This whole theory about a balloon is pretty farfetched, don't you think? I mean, this is coming from me."

"How about we ask him?" Bert said, walking toward the crime scene again.

CAROLYN Q. HUNTER

Chapter 9

Much to Bert's frustration, Detective Mannor wasn't buying her newest theory, but to humor her, he took the balloon into evidence anyway. He informed her that the possibility of the killer shooting from the street, hitting a balloon, and managing to hit the victim—all without someone noticing—was a long shot. Carla had worn an *I told you so* kind of smirk as they walked back to *Christmas in July.*

Soon after, Bert headed home for the night, exhausted from the day's events—and not too thrilled about her idea being shot down.

* * *

Upon waking up the next morning, she realized just how silly her little theory was and felt ridiculous for bringing the detective a useless balloon fragment.

Trying to shrug it off, she decided to treat herself to something nice on the way into work that day. Thinking of the delightful smell of the detective's pumpkin spice coffee from the night before, she located a convenient *Koffee Hous* in the downtown area.

The coffee shop was on the main level of a high-rise office building on one of the corners. The familiar logo of a smiling woman, cup of coffee in hand, against a black background jumped out from the window.

Parking on the street (and being thankful that the paid meters didn't start until after nine) she headed inside. Instantly, the warming sensation of the shop overwhelmed her. A mixture of cinnamon, pumpkin, and coffee grounds permeated the air.

An elegant, yet modern design included black tables and counter, stools, and soft light fixtures.

Unfortunately, the atmosphere was immediately broken up by the angry demands of some young woman at the front of the line. "You're going to do as I say, or I'll make sure you get fired."

"I-I'm sorry, ma'am, but any extra shots of cream or flavoring cost more," the timid young woman behind the counter muttered.

"I'm sure you don't want me to get your manager, do you?" she demanded.

In the next instant, Bert recognized the woman. It was Abigail, Charles Blinkerton's daughter. She wore a well fitted black pencil skirt, a crushed velvet blouse, and a pair of expensive sunglasses. Her hair was pinned up with what looked like a crystal hair stick.

Her overall appearance was completely different, more grown up, than the day before.

What was she doing here? Getting a casual cup of coffee, the day after her own father was murdered?

"I don't have any control over this. It's our store policy."

"Then maybe it's time we changed that policy, hmm?" she said in as condescending a tone as possible, looking over the tops of her sunglasses with scathing eyes.

Bert couldn't believe the woman's behavior toward the poor barista. She often found issue with anyone who thought they were better than the everyday workers who strived to give the public what they needed. She was sure working a barista job wasn't the girl's favorite thing, and having a rude customer come in always just made things worse.

Abigail was also acting differently. Yes, the rudeness, and greediness were still there, but any semblance of the ditzy innocence or childish youth had vanished.

"Should I get the manager then?" the barista asked, clearly unaware of what to do next in the situation.

"You'd better. And pray that they are far more lenient than I would be," she shouted as the girl headed off.

She wondered if the poor woman was just upset about her father's murder and was taking it out on other people. It was a strong likelihood. Bert remembered losing her husband, Howie, and how she'd been so snappy and rude for the few weeks following. She'd had to make a lot of apologies after that.

She decided to give her the benefit of the doubt and stepped forward. "Abigail?"

The woman did a double take, surprised to hear her own name spoken. "Yes?"

"I just wanted to say, I'm so sorry about your father."

"And who are you?" she demanded, lowered her glasses to the tip of her nose and sending daggers at Bert. She clearly didn't remember the incident outside the pie shop the day before—or at least didn't recognize Bert.

"I'm the owner of the pie shop, where you and your father stopped yesterday," she reminded her.

Her jaw dropped open. "Then it's your place where my father was murdered!" she exclaimed, her voice bouncing off the ceiling.

"I'm afraid so."

She shoved her glasses back up on her nose. "You're lucky I'm not calling the police right now."

Bert's breath caught in her throat. "Excuse me?"

"I could have you arrested for harassment, you know."

Bert took a step back. "I have no idea what you mean."

"You're following me?"

"I'm doing no such thing."

"Probably trying to kill me, too?"

"I sure I have no idea what you're talking about?"

"I don't know. Maybe it's the fact that two men have been killed at your shop."

Bert was shocked, unconsciously taking a step back from the woman's verbal accusation.

"That's right. I looked it up. What are you, some old murderous woman who gets her kicks by knocking off poor lonely men like my father?"

"Excuse me," Bert snapped. "I have done no such thing, and you have no right to blame me. I simply wanted to offer my condolences."

"Save your breath for the courtroom," she held up a hand silencing her.

Either this woman was simply delusional, or she was purposefully manipulative and vindictive.

A second later, the coffee shop's manager appeared. "What seems to be the problem, ma'am?"

Abagail turned with a furtive brow. "Your staff refuses to give me two extra shots of cream and syrup free of charge."

The manager tilted his head knowingly. "Well, our policy is to charge for extras like that, ma'am. My employee was only following my instructions."

"I should have known as much. Don't you worry. I can see to it you lose your job as well if I don't like the way I'm treated," she barked.

"You'll have to contact the district manager for that," he noted.

"I intend to." Standing up straight, she jutted her nose in the air. "I'm going to own you, all of you," she threatened.

Bert couldn't help but let her jaw drop again in shock.

Turning on her expensive heel, Abigail faced Bert one last time. "I'm sure I'll see you in court when this murder comes to trial."

With a flip of her hair, she waltzed past her and out the door.

"Sorry about that," the manager sighed.

Bert walked up to the counter. "It's nothing you could control, I'm sure. Do you get customers like that often?"

"She's been coming in every day for the last few weeks, acting rude, like she owns the place," the timid barista admitted.

"She acts like that every day?" Bert gasped.

"Worse sometimes. She seems to think we all owe her some great debt or something," the manager confessed, shaking his head.

"I'm so sorry to hear that."

"Never mind that. How about a drink on the house?" he offered.

"That sounds lovely."

"Great. What'll it be?"

Bert smiled. "I'd love to try the pumpkin spice coffee, please."

Chapter 10

Finally arriving at *Pies and Pages*, all the while delightedly sipping her festive coffee, Bert parked her car and got out. As she approached the front of her shop, she paused. For a moment, she was sure that Abigail Blinketon was standing outside the front door, staring up at the windows.

"Oh, great. What does she want now?" Bert grumbled, not in the mood to be accused or berated anymore.

Honestly, what possible reason could she have for killing a stranger like Daniel Blinkerton? It was simply ludicrous. Why was Abigail jumping to such wild conclusions?

As she got closer, however, Bert realized it wasn't Abigail at all— just someone who had a similar stance. She was an older woman whose hair had begun to gray along the edges. Her figure, however, seemed to be too perfectly preserved and Bert secretly wondered if there had been any elective surgery involved.

"Good morning. Can I help you?" she greeted the woman.

"Oh," she exclaimed, turning with a start and placing her hand at her throat. A pinkish hue invaded her cheeks.

"I'm sorry. I didn't mean to scare you."

"Quite alright, dear. It's my fault completely. I was lost in thought."

"If you're looking to get a slice of pie, I'm afraid that I don't open until ten. I haven't even started the baking yet. If you're just looking for a book, though, I'm more than happy to let you in a little early to browse."

"No, no, nothing like that." She turned back with a wistful look in her eyes, examining the shop front.

"Then what is it, ma'am?"

"Oh, I'm sure this sounds silly, but my ex-husband just died yesterday. I'm sure you're already aware, because he was shot right here."

"You're Daniel Blinkerton's ex-wife?"

"That I am. Soria Blinkerton," she introduced herself.

Bert stepped forward holding out a hand. "My name is Bert Hannah.

"Did you know him, my ex-husband I mean?"

"Not at all. I only met him and your two children yesterday during the Autumn Walk."

The woman shook her head. "Those children. Still living at home with their father, I assume, like two little parasites. I never did know what to do with either of them, especially that girl." The mother turned slightly pale as she spoke of the past, almost as if she didn't like thinking of it.

Was this woman indicating that she didn't like her own children? Bert hesitated. "I wouldn't know."

She let out a small laugh. "Neither would I. I haven't had any real contact with them in the last two years."

"Really?" Bert asked, trying not to sound too judgmental.

"They both have . . . problems. The boy is spineless and the girl . . . well, she's something else altogether. I wanted no part of their lives, anymore."

"I see," she responded, a little awkwardly.

"Trust me, if you knew the history, you'd be on board with me," Soria noted, having read Bert's expression.

"Oh, I'm not one to judge someone else's situation or choices. It just surprised me is all."

"Look, after spending over twenty years in a house with a man who argued with me at every turn, condescended my choices, treated me like I was less just because I was a woman, I had to get out of there. The kids' problems—good heavens—were just sort of the kicker, ya' know?"

Bert paused, surprised about how blatantly open this woman seemed to be about her personal problems. She'd met types like this before, a few at her church, who took any opportunity to share their own personal sorrow.

She decided it would only be polite to offer the woman an ear for a few minutes, if that's what she needed. She motioned to the door. "Would you like to come in for a cup of coffee, maybe a slice of pie once I get the first one made? On the house."

Blinking in surprise, the woman smiled. "You're serious?"

Bert shrugged. "We all need a friend sometimes."

"In that case, I'd love to."

"Great." Unlocking the door, she led the way inside.

"I appreciate this. I've just finished a long drive through the night to be here."

"You drove here?"

She nodded. "From Wyoming. I guess the kids gave that Detective my information, heaven knows how they had it. Anyway, he calls me up and tells me there's been a murder and he wants to ask me some questions. I offered to drive in to talk to him in person."

"Wow, that's impressive." Bert walked behind the counter and scooped two tablespoons of coffee into the machine.

"I was married to the man, for heaven's sake. Even if I didn't like him, I thought I owed him the respect of coming down this way."

Turning on the pot, Bert walked to the freezer and pulled out another set of pastry dough she'd prepared ahead of time. "And your kids?"

She sighed. "I guess there's no getting around it. I'll have to see them at some point while I'm here."

Sprinkling some flour onto the counter, Bert laid the dough down and grabbed her rolling pin. "Do you *want* to see them?"

There was a pause while the woman thought. "I suppose, some part of me does. As a mother, you always have a connection with your children, even if you can't stand them. What kind of adult child lives at home well into their twenties?"

"Well, day to day costs are more than they used to be," Bert offered.

She scoffed. "Still, have some respect. Of course, Daniel enables them like crazy—especially Abigail. He always gave her whatever she wanted, spoiled her. It was his way of trying to make up for her problems, I guess." She shook her head, sneering in disgust. "He just made things worse. Meanwhile, he purposefully tied Charleston down, never let him get a leg up. I couldn't say or do anything to fix it."

Bert rolled out the dough into a flat round. Grabbing a ceramic pie plate from the cupboard, she placed it upside down on top of the dough and then flipped the whole thing over, letting the crust settle into the dish.

"Anyway, I'd finally had it and just up and left. That was two years ago."

"And you haven't seen any of them since?"

Taking a seat at an empty table, she shook her head. "No."

"But you drove through the night to come here today?"

"That's right. Like I said, I feel like I owe them something, even if it's small. I won't stay long. I'll give my statement, maybe say hello to my children to save face, and then be on my way back to Wyoming—back to my new life." She waved a hand at the window. "I walked away from all of this years ago."

Bert couldn't help but wonder at this strange family dynamic. In some way, she could see Abigail's bad attitude being a result of both her parents. On the other hand, Soria seemed outwardly more genial than her daughter.

"Well, it looks like you're doing well for yourself," Bert commented as she trimmed the edges of the crust and slipped it into the oven while it heated.

Soria looked down at her hand, at the expensive rings and watch there. "Yes, single life has treated me very well. I was finally able to start using that law degree I got all those years back."

"You studied law?" The coffee pot finished filling and Bert poured two mugs.

"When I was much younger, yes. Then I met Daniel and he wanted to start a family, wanted me to stay home. I was foolish and young and believed it was for the best. Luckily, I had an old college friend up in Casper. Despite years not using my experience, he got me an entry job at his firm."

Setting the mugs down, Bert took a seat.

As soon as she had, there was a loud knock on the door. Looking up, Bert was surprised to see Detective Mannor standing outside impatiently.

Hopping back up, she opened the door. "Morning, Detective."

"Is Soria Blinkerton here?"

Bert's jaw dropped open. How did he know that? "She is. Why?"

Without another word, the large man had pushed his way into the shop and over to the table. "Soria Blinkerton?"

Blinking in astonishment, she glanced up. "Yes?"

"I'm going to need you to come down to the station with me."

"Oh, I'll be glad to. I was going to head over there right after this. Let me just finish my coffee."

"No, now."

She gasped, putting her palm flat on the table. "Now? That's rude, Detective."

"Either come willingly now, or I'll place you under arrest."

"Place me under arrest? What for? I hope you don't mean for my ex-husband's murder."

He was silent for a second, not answering the question.

"But, I wasn't even here in town. How can you even think to charge me?"

"I'm not . . . yet."

"Like I said, I wasn't even here."

"I wouldn't be so sure of that, ma'am. We have sources that say otherwise."

She sat with her mouth hanging open for a moment, but finally stood up. "Very, well. I'll come along." Heading for the door, she turned to Bert. "Do you mind contacting my son about this?"

"Me?" Bert protested.

"Yes, he'll need to know what is going on. He's probably the only one who'll be willing to help if it comes to it." Digging in her purse, Soria pulled out a notepad with an address already scribbled on it. "Here is the address. Thanks."

Then they walked out the door.

Chapter 11

Bert wasn't sure how she got roped into these situations. If it were up to her, she'd lead a simple and quiet life, baking pies and selling books—not getting dragged into one murder case after another. The whole thing seemed ridiculous.

Still, she was a woman of honor and decency, and felt it was only right to do as Soria had asked, even though they had just met.

She'd offered the coffee and pie in good conscience, thinking that a woman who had just lost a loved one—even if it was an ex—might like a little comfort.

There were a few little things that did confuse her, however, as she looked at the sticky note. Why did she have a pre-prepared address written down in her purse? It was almost as if she had planned on the possibility of being arrested, knowing she'd need to pass the note off at the last second.

On top of the note, what the detective had said was confusing. Soria had been there in town during the murder, even though she'd specifically said that she drove through the night to be there? That alone wasn't reason enough for arrest. So, what else was missing from this formula?

Bert arrived outside the small house around nine, having rushed to get the morning pies done and in the warmer before dashing off to see this young man she'd hardly met to bring him news about family matters she knew little about. If she was fast, she could see the son— Charleston was his name—and make it back to the shop in time for opening. Parking on the street, she got out and walked up the sidewalk to the door.

Knocking, she waited anxiously while tapping her foot.

A minute later, the door opened. "Yes? Can I help you?" the young man asked without opening the screen.

"Hi, my name is Bert Hannah. We met briefly yesterday."

Charleston narrowed his eyes, scanning her features. "Hey, wait a minute. You're the lady from the pie shop."

Bert smiled awkwardly. "Yep. That's me."

Charleston's face turned grim. "What do you want? I'm done talking about my father's murder." He went to close the door.

Bert held up one finger for him to wait. "Hold on."

"What do you want?"

"I'm actually here about your mother, not your father."

This caused him to pause, his brow furrowing in confusion. "My mother? What about her?"

"She asked me to come and tell you that she was taken down to the police station this morning. She happened to be at my shop when it happened and I was the only person around to bring you the message."

Charleston stepped forward and opened the screen. "You mean she was arrested?"

By the tone of his voice, Bert couldn't help but wonder if he already knew his mother was hanging around. He clearly showed little to no surprise about the fact that his own estranged mom was in town after two years.

"Not exactly, but the detective did take her in for questioning. He threatened to arrest her if she didn't come willingly."

"He can't do that," the young man argued.

"He can, and he has."

"What for? She hasn't done anything wrong," his voice was raising higher and higher with each sentence, and his face was beginning to redden.

"According to the detective, there are witnesses who saw her here in town yesterday, which means she would have been around during the time of the murder."

Charleston's face drooped in shock. "No, no way."

Bert hesitated. "What is it?"

"Dang," he sighed, leaning on the door jamb. "You say she sent you?"

"That's right. Just to tell you what's going on."

"You better come in for a second." Stepping aside, he motioned for her to step past the threshold.

Bert hesitated. "Okay," she agreed a little reluctantly, not wanting to get dragged into this family drama any more than she already had been. Glancing into the corner, she noticed a fabric rifle case sitting there. It was empty.

Had the murder weapon come from this very house? That made Bert nervous to be alone with the young man.

Closing the door behind himself, Charleston moved into the musty living room. He was audibly mumbling nonsense as he passed into the room. "She must have seen us. I just know it."

"Who?" Bert pressed.

"My sister. Abigail."

Bert shook her head, a little lost at this point, and took a seat on the couch. "Why don't you start at the beginning?"

Charleston groaned. "Okay, well you see, I've been trying to get up enough funds to go to the community college here in town." He began pacing the floor at this point, anxious as he told the story.

"Okay?" Bert said, still not seeing how anything he'd said was relevant or made any sense without some sort of context.

"I originally asked my dad for the money, and he blatantly told me no. He said it was a complete waste of time and effort and that I didn't have enough talent."

"Wow."

"He claimed he didn't have the money, but I knew he was full of it. He's always buying stuff for Abigail. She was the favorite."

Bert knew that little tidbit of information just based on the one uncomfortable encounter they'd all had outside the shop the day before.

"I mean, I know she was sick when we were younger, but does that mean she deserves all the attention?"

"She was sick?"

"I'd say so. My mom and dad were always taking her off to the doctor when we were in middle school."

"And you don't know what it was?"

"Nope. They never told me. Anyway, I knew I shouldn't have asked him in the first place. He never supported me in anything I've ever done or wanted to do. He's always trying to put me in my place, told me I needed to just go get a job bagging groceries or flipping burgers because it was all I'd ever be good at."

Even as he spoke about it, the same red agitation arose in his cheeks. This was clearly a long-standing issue that affected his entire life.

"So, my next step was to figure it out on my own. I did research on student loan options, even printed out an application for one."

"That's a sensible choice," she agreed.

"But he found the application and shredded it. He told me he wouldn't allow me to go to school if he could help it. Claimed he'd just end up paying my loans."

"But you're a legal adult, correct? He had no real power to stop you."

"You don't know my father," he whispered, just the memory of the man causing sweat to run down Charleston's face.

"When was this?"

"Two nights ago. We really had it out, and then I left for the shooting range."

"The shooting range?" she instantly felt her heart skip a beat. Wondering if she should try and get out of there, Bert moved to the edge of her seat.

The hint of a tear appeared in his eye. "Y-yeah. There is an indoor shooting range near here where I sometimes go to blow off steam." A sniffle escaped, and he drew back in any sign of crying, obviously adept at hiding it. "Shooting guns was the one thing my dad actually did with me. He taught me."

Bert paused, wondering if she should ask the next question on her mind. "Are you a good shot?"

He nodded. "Thanks to him, I'm one of the best," he bragged.

"I see."

"Anyway, while I was out I got to thinking about Mom."

"You hadn't seen her in a couple years, right?"

"That's true, but I did manage to track her down at one-point a while back. I've sort of e-mailed back and forth with her for a while."

That was one tidbit of information Soria hadn't shared. By the way she talked, you'd think she'd never even humor her kids. More and more it seemed she still had a soft spot—at least for Charleston.

"I called her up and told her about what had happened, asked her for the money." He was quiet for the next moment, leaving Bert in suspense.

"And?"

"She agreed to help me pay for college on one condition, that I move out of my father's house once and for all. She wanted me out from under his reign and control."

"I see. Did she offer to mail the money? Transfer it?"

"No. She didn't trust my Dad. He might see the letter first and get rid of it or take it for himself."

Finally, Bert understood. "She offered to come out and meet you in person."

"We'd moved since she left, sort of Dad's way of making sure she couldn't find us, and I gave her the address."

That explained the note in her purse.

"She told me she was going to drive through the night to be here yesterday morning."

"And was she here?"

He hesitated, not sure if sharing the truth would be incriminating.

"I'm not the police. You can tell me."

"She did come, but Abigail must have seen us together."

Bert sighed, shaking her head. "Most likely, she's the one who told the police your mother was here in town."

Finally, after having paced the floor, Charleston sat down. "At this point, the money doesn't matter. I'm taking over my father's investments and will, therefore, have control of the money."

Bert tilted her head. She hadn't known there was any money involved. If Charleston stood to take over, it gave him a motive. Bert moved closer to the edge of her chair. "What kind of investments?"

"I'm not sure, exactly. I won't find out right away until all the paperwork has officially gone through, but I know his will leaves them in my hands. I guess that was the one benefit of being a man in his eyes. If he had to choose between Abigail and me to take his money after he died, he chose me."

This didn't surprise Bert.

"He never talked about his work?"

"He was always starting some project or another—mostly fast food chains and stuff like that. One time he bought into a burger chain. Unfortunately, the location he owned went under and he lost money." Charleston shrugged. "He must have made at least one good investment. How else would he have the cash to buy an expensive pie on a whim? No offense."

"None taken." Standing up, Bert slid her purse back onto her shoulder, wanting nothing more than to get out of there. Charleston seemed timid, but that didn't mean he wasn't capable of murder.

"You're leaving?" he asked, a hint of vulnerability in his voice.

"I have to open up my pie shop for the day." Her voice faltered slightly, but she caught it.

"You're still opening your shop after what happened?" he demanded, the rosiness returning to his face.

"I still have a business to run."

He sighed heavily, leaning down and folding his arms. "I thought you'd at least come to the police station with me, since my mom sent you and all."

These two kids really were strange, just like Soria had said.

"No, I have to talk to someone."

Chapter 12

Bert barely made it back to the shop to open on time. Stepping inside, the smell of freshly baked pies greeted her. The scent alone, along with the warmth of the ovens, brought a sense of peace after the crazy morning she'd had.

She'd had to deal with three of the Blinkerton clan. Each of them had been so vastly different, but somehow the same.

Abigail was rude, demanding, and overbearing.

Soria was genial, but told white lies.

Charleston was a little weak in the spine and acted the part of a martyr.

However, Bert realized that any one of them could have resorted to murder if they felt they deserved something they weren't getting.

The question now was, who would be desperate enough to do it?

For all Bert knew, Detective Mannor already had the right person in mind. Surely there was some sort of condemning evidence that had come up to point to her. Of course, showing up randomly after two years was odd on its own, but the fact that the murder had happened the same day seemed far more than coincidence.

Still, Bert had a hunch and she wanted to follow through on a few things to help pinpoint exactly where she thought this whole ordeal might be going.

She only hoped her day went according to plan.

Even after only being open for a week, she already had a few regulars who stopped in for their daily slice of pie. Some were ladies who enjoyed a dessert during their lunch break, others were men who stopped in for a relaxing bite after work.

It was only a handful, but Bert was proud of it.

One of those consistent regulars was a man named Marc Bailey, a local businessman and investor who had acquired a fondness for Bert's fabulous apple pie. It also helped that Bert had inadvertently lent him a hand previously—getting him out of a very sticky situation during a murder investigation. Afterwards, Marc had grown fond of Bert, and even considered her a friend despite his normal outward seriousness.

He always arrived around four in the afternoon for his scheduled slice of pure sugary cinnamon and apple bliss.

Bert worked straight through the day, rolling out pies and making book recommendations, all to take her mind off the recent murder and the odd family drama attached to it. While the book side of things hadn't really picked up steam yet, she had hoped to get more interest by her sidewalk sales. She also had plans up her sleeve to get the whole reading community involved.

Nothing seemed to beat a good read on a chilly autumn day, and she was formulating an advertising scheme to interest guests in possibly picking up a new book to read in addition to their slice of delicious pie.

As four o'clock drew near, Bert was relieved to see Marc approaching the front door of the shop. He wore a black knit cap over his long blonde hair, which matched his expensive and well-tailored business suit. It was partially to keep it from flying out in the wind, and partially to keep his ears warm.

His ruddy cheeks and foggy breath were simple indications that the days were progressively getting colder.

"Hi, Marc," Bert smiled upon seeing him.

"Hey," he beamed, flashing her the winning all-tooth smile that she'd come to associate with the man. "It's colder than a witch's tit in an iron bra out there," he joked, removing the cap and revealing that his hair was tied up in a bun.

Bert couldn't help but laugh at his crass humor. In some part, it reminded her of her late husband's ridiculous jokes. "I've got your apple pie all ready for you."

Walking up to the glass display counter, he leaned in and looked at the other choices. "I was actually thinking of trying something different today," he noted in his usual New York accent.

"You? Have something other than apple pie? I thought it was your favorite?"

"It is, but sometimes you've got to branch out."

She laughed again. Even though he was in his thirties and Bert was in her sixties, she couldn't help but feel that he was a kindred spirit—despite her poor first impression of him during the prior murder investigation.

"Okay, what'll you have?"

"I've been hearing rave reviews around the *Old Market* that your chocolate-almond tart is to die for."

"You want to give that a try?"

"Yes, ma'am."

"One slice of chocolate-almond tart coming right up."

He began undoing his black scarf. "Could I get a cup of coffee with that? I think if I don't get something warm in me soon I'm going to turn into a popsicle."

"It isn't even winter yet, Marc. How will you survive?"

"I won't," he grinned.

"Didn't you grow up in New York?" she asked, filling a mug with delicious hot liquid.

"Yep, and thank heaven the winters aren't nearly as miserable here in Nebraska."

"Here you go," Bert offered, setting the cup of hot coffee on the glass counter.

"You're a life saver, as always." He took it in both hands, letting its heat warm him. Sipping from the mug, he took a seat at the closest table.

"Speaking of saving lives," Bert's voice trailed off as she got the pie out of the heated display case and cut a slice. She paused, already feeling slightly awkward.

"What is it?" he asked, knowing there was something she wanted to ask.

"You're in investing, right?" she walked over and set the pie on the table in front of him.

"Of course. You already knew that, though." He picked up the fork and cut into the pie.

"I did."

"So, what is it? Looking for advice?" He took a bite. An instant look of happiness washed over him. "Oh, my. This might be better than your apple."

"Thanks," she smiled. "What kind of investing are you in?"

"Stocks and bonds mostly."

"Have you ever bought into a fast food chain?"

He took another bite and finished chewing it before answering. "I've run stock with them before, but that's not what you mean, is it?"

"No. I was thinking more along the lines of actually buying a location, a franchise. Being an owner."

"I've never done that, no."

"Darn," she sighed.

"Why?"

"I was just wondering if there was a way to find out who owns which of the locations of *Koffee Hous* in town."

"*Koffee Hous*? They're a pretty huge chain." Sipping his coffee again, he considered this fact. "I suppose you could always talk to the district manager. He'll probably know who the owners were."

"You think that's doable?"

"I know the district manager, if that helps."

"It does," she exclaimed.

"Why do you need to know, by the way?"

Bert folded her arms over her frilly red and black apron. "I just have a hunch about something and I'm trying to verify it."

"Okay. I'll drop him a line tonight and have him call you."

"That sounds wonderful, thank you," she gushed, truly hoping she would be able to settle things once and for all.

"*Koffee Hous* is a huge chain. I bet you'd make bank owning one of those places, if you were smart about it."

"What exactly does an owner do. They aren't the manager, are they?"

"No, no. They don't have to do much of anything. They take care of water and electric bills for the building, repairs, things like that, but many of them aren't very hands on. That's up to the store manager."

"I see." She moved over back behind the counter.

"In any case, I hope you figure out whatever it is you're looking for."

"Me, too," she agreed.

Chapter 13

I t wasn't until eight that same evening, just as Bert was locking the front door to the shop, that her phone began to ring. Making sure the deadbolt was firmly set, she rushed back behind the counter and picked up her phone from where it sat vibrating on the messy cooking counter, creating wafts of flour in the air.

"*Pies and Pages*, this is Bert speaking. How may I help you?"

"Hi, Bert. This is Thomas Raisin, the district manager of *Koffee Hous* in Culver's Hood, Nebraska."

"Oh, Mr. Raisin, thank you for calling on such short notice. I really appreciate it." Bert tried to multitask while talking, using a damp rag to begin wiping up the loose flour on the counter.

"Of course. I'm more than happy to make a business call, even on a late evening such as this. Marc Bailey dropped me a line and told me to ring you up."

"Yes, as a matter of fact, I asked him for a favor," she admitted, shaking the cloth out over the sink.

"Well, a friend of Marc's is a friend of mine. I understand you're interested in buying one of our locations."

Bert hesitated, realizing that there might have been a miscommunication somewhere along the way.

"Mrs. Hannah? Are you still there?"

"Yes. Yes, I am. I'm sorry, but I think you may have misunderstood."

He paused, the sound of his breathing increasing slightly. "So, you're not interested in investing in one of our locations?"

"I'm sorry, no."

"I see. Then it seems we have nothing further to discuss," he noted with a sharp clip of the tongue.

"Actually, I was hoping to get some information on the people who currently are investors in Culver's Hood."

There was a curious hum over the line. "Am I correct in my understanding that you own a pie shop in *Old Market*?"

"Yes, that's correct," she answered, not sure exactly what this had to do with the situation at hand.

"And you sell coffee there?"

"Of course. Sometimes my customers want something warm to drink with their pie."

"Then, I can also assume you are interested in hearing about our current sales numbers, maybe even our business practices?" he accused, his voice growing gravelly.

"What? Not at all."

"I realize you're a minor, start-up business, and we are a large corporation. However, we in no way can share any information about our sales numbers, marketing, or any other aspect of our business plan—even with a quaint little shop like yours."

She set the rag down and put her free hand on her hip. "Excuse me," she barked, not appreciating his condescending tone. She'd never taken flak from overbearing businessmen before, and she wasn't about to start now.

"I'm sorry, Mrs. Hannah, but this conversation is over."

"No, it is far from over," she ordered, her face growing hot from anger. She couldn't believe the nerve of this man, assuming she was attempting to do some shady investigations of the competition. Heck, she hardly considered them competition at all.

"Goodbye."

"Now, hold on just a darn minute, you. All I sell is plain black coffee. Customers can add their own sugar or cream if they like, but I don't have the menu or choices to rival yours."

"My point exactly."

"But I do sell delicious pie, which your company does not."

"Mrs. Hannah, we sell a number of baked goods. I'm sure you understand."

"Will you listen to me, for crying out loud?"

There was a distinct pause on the line. Bert figured the district manager wasn't used to being spoken to in such a manner. A man in his position likely had store managers, employees, and other *peons* bowing down to him every day.

"I have no interest in learning the ins and outs of your business, your finances, your sales numbers, or anything else of the sort. I'm simple business woman with a simple dream and am trying to serve people pie and books, not because I'm looking to make a million bucks, but because I love it."

She swore she could hear a coughing noise, probably a scoff at her passionate speech.

"My point is, I'm trying to get some simple information," she sucked in air through her mouth, realizing she hadn't breathed during her little tirade.

"And what, exactly, is that?"

"Who is the owner of the location on Third and Downhue?"

There was another moment of silence as Mr. Raisin thought. "And that's the only thing you're looking to know?"

"Yes, it is."

He sighed contemptuously. "All right. I think I can accommodate that request."

"Thank you. I apologize for snapping."

"It is quite all right. I made some incorrect assumptions on my end," he admitted, even though his voice sounded pained to do it.

"That's fine. Just a miscommunication, I'm sure."

There was a shuffle of papers and the click of a computer mouse. "Now, if I remember correctly, the owner at that location is very hands off. I'm not sure he has once ever set foot on the property. Whenever there was an issue, plumbing, heating, that sort of thing, he simply hired someone to go in and look at it without him being there."

If Bert was correct in her assumptions, this wasn't surprising.

"Still, he's been the owner there for nearly ten years." Another few mouse clocks echoed over the line. "Ah, yes. Here it is. I'm not sure I've met this man except for one time."

"And what is his name?" Bert pressed.

"His name is Daniel Blinkerton."

Chapter 14

Rushing to finish up the closing duties—including cleaning everything and packing up any leftover pie to take to her church's youth group later in the week—Bert threw on her jacket and headed out the door.

She had intentions of walking down to the police station, which was only a few blocks away in the downtown area, and discussing what she had learned with Detective Mannor. If she was correct in her assumptions, Daniel Blinkerton's ex-wife in no way benefited financially from his death.

Wrapping her scarf tightly around her neck, she headed down the nearly deserted street. Only the occasional car puttered by. Most of the shops were closed for the evening, or were in the process of closing, dimming many of their lights or drawing the shades—casting shadows out into the night.

The old street lamps still sent off a comforting glow as Bert walked along. Additionally, the moon granted some small light to the quiet historic downtown area. Glancing up, Bert could almost feel the holiday season upon them.

In a matter of weeks, it would be Halloween and she would be serving festive dishes to trick or treaters of all ages. She was looking forward to celebrating all the holidays from her little shop. It was a wonderful time of life that she wouldn't get back again, like so many other special times before.

Taking a moment to hop down into the gutter, she kicked at the dry leaves resting there the way she always had when she was young. The crunch was so undeniably satisfying. A small wind blew through the streets, creating a swirling dance of leaves around her feet.

Despite the warmth of her scarf, she began to wish she'd carried a knit cap with her as well, because her ears were beginning to get chilled.

The gust came down off the buildings, sweeping the street and carrying the leaves upward toward the darkness of the night sky above her.

Bert stopped and watched mother nature's dance, glad to have the moment of quiet in all the chaos of the last few days. She cherished her times alone as much as her time with friends.

Then, something strange caught her eye.

A glint of moonlight seemed to be penetrating down upon her, almost as if it were being concentrated into a single beam. Blinking, she held up one hand and saw a small circle of light appear on her palm—almost as if she were holding it.

Following the path of the beam, she looked up at the wooden sign over the toy store. There appeared to be a rather small hole, a perfect circle, through the O in *FunWorld*. Bert just happened to be standing in exactly the right position for the moonlight to shine through it on her.

"How did that happen?" she wondered out loud.

Walking over so she was just beneath the sign, she looked up at it and tried to make sense of what she was seeing. It was difficult from below on the sidewalk to make out any real details.

She glanced around for any way to get closer, and noticed the tree nearby. It had a wrought iron fence surrounding the trunk. She figured she could at least step up on that for a closer look, just so long as no one saw her.

It certainly would be odd to see a sixty-year-old woman climbing a tree late at night in the middle of the *Old Market.*

Double checking she was alone, Bert hoisted one foot onto the first rung of the fence, and then the next, balancing herself against the trunk.

She was only up there a couple of seconds, but it was enough to get a good look at the strange hole.

Suddenly, she realized what she was looking at.

It was a clean-cut bullet hole.

Based on the angle at which the bullet seemed to pass through, it looked like the shot had come from somewhere high up. Bert, climbed down and quickly shuffled over back to the spot where the moon shone through. Looking up, she saw the yellow crescent over a four-story brownstone apartment building.

Whoever had killed Daniel Blinkerton, had sniped him from the roof.

Chapter 15

Bert didn't hesitate for a single second, heading toward the old building. She had to at least stand up there and make sure her assumptions were correct before running off to Detective Mannor with another theory. If she didn't have at least some sort of evidence, he wouldn't even give her the time of day.

Not after the balloon incident.

Now, however, the idea that the balloon popped because of the bullet seemed like more of a possibility.

Reaching the building, she saw that the first floor was made up of storefronts, mostly restaurants. The three floors above that were apartments. Walking to the center glass doors, with the stairs leading to floors above, she pulled on the handle and stepped inside.

Jogging to the foot of the steps, she began climbing up and up toward the top. She tried to be quiet and discreet, so as not spook anyone in the apartments. Many of the units were quiet, but a few had the sound of television echoing from inside.

Reaching the final landing, Bert noticed two doors. One was marked as a supply closet and the other led out to the roof. Stepping through the metal doorway, she found herself back outside in the chilly autumn air.

Even more than the streets below, the flat expanse around her was dark. No street lamps or emergency lights illuminated the area. Reaching into her purse, she pulled out her mini flashlight she always kept on her keys and turned it on.

Using the knowledge her late husband had taught her about hunting, and about shooting prey from afar, she tried to put two and two together. The spot where the shot would have likely come from was the far corner, just behind a large electrical generator.

Walking across the roof and slipping into the small space there, she looked over the edge. Sure enough, she could see the exact spot in front of her shop where Daniel had died—and the toy store sign was right in between.

She needed to tell Detective Mannor about this right away. Suddenly, she felt something hard under her shoe. Lifting her foot, she gasped. Laying on the concrete was the bullet casing of a single shell. Carefully, she picked it up and slipped it into her purse for the detective.

This was undeniable proof that the killer had shot the gun from up here.

Spinning around to run back down the fire escape, Bert stopped suddenly in her tracks as the barrel of a gun was pointed in her face.

"Don't move a muscle," the assailant threatened.

Chapter 16

"Abigail," Bert exclaimed, putting up her hands to show she didn't want any trouble.

"Did you find what you were looking for?" she asked.

Bert blinked, looking at the gun pointed right at her heart. "No. I had no idea what I might find until I saw the shell just now." She instantly regretted what she said. She'd basically just admitted she had evidence that the shooting took place from the roof.

"Don't lie. You knew you'd find something up here, didn't you?"

Bert shook her head again. "I swear, I didn't. I just was seeing if the shot could really be made from here."

Abigail pursed her lips. "Very astute, I suppose. I knew you were going to be trouble when you I caught you spying on me at the coffee shop, today," Abigail Blinkerton sneered, jabbing the gun at Bert.

"The coffee shop? You mean at the *Koffee Hous*?"

"That's right," she snapped, raising her lip on one side and showing her teeth like a snarling dog.

"I wasn't following you. I just wanted to pick up a pumpkin spice coffee."

She jabbed the gun into Bert's chest. "A likely story, I'm sure. You were trying to find some evidence that I did in my old dad."

Bert shrugged nervously, trying not to show just how shaken she was by the gun trained on her. "I-I'll admit. Your attitude with the employees this morning did tip me off. I'd only ever met you the few times, out in front of my shop and at the coffee shop. I thought your behavior in both instances was a little odd. At my shop, you went from sweet to snappy and nasty in a matter of seconds."

"Of course, I did. My dad wasn't giving me what I wanted," she growled, bearing her teeth.

"Then you were acting like you owned the place at the coffee shop. I remembered your father arguing about money and investments with your brother. It was a long shot, so I did a little digging. Your father owned one of the local branches of *Koffee Hous.*"

Abigail nodded, never taking her eye off the rifle's sights. "That he did. He thought I was soooo stupid. Poor, dear, little ol' me could never figure out anything about investments or money," she said in a mocking voice. "But about a month ago, I found out, and I knew that's where most of his money was coming from."

"That's when you started visiting that location every day, treating the employees terribly. Is that when you started planning all of this?"

"Perhaps," she whispered.

"Not even Charleston knew exactly what your father had invested."

"Because he was a simple-minded idiot who only had dreams of studying music."

"But why kill your father? You should have known he was going to leave everything to your brother as the man of the family."

Her grip tightened on the stock, her fingers turning red, then white, with the pressure. "That's why I used my brother's gun, of course. I thought for sure they could trace the bullet back to him and peg him as the murderer. Once he was locked away, I'd be in control."

"But it didn't work out? I'm guessing you were nearly interrupted while you were up here and had to leave the gun behind on the roof while you made your escape?"

"Even though I used my brother's old jacket to muffle the noise, and used the balloon as cover, someone heard the shot. I was forced to drop the gun here, hidden behind the box, and then dash down the stairs and hide in a supply closet until they were gone."

"You must be quite the shot."

She smirked. "The best in the family, no thanks to my overbearing father. I snuck out all the time to practice shooting on my own. I read books in secret on the subject, got men I met at the firing range to help teach me."

Bert nodded. "I thought as much. That book you asked for the other day was a very advanced manual, nothing for beginners."

Abigail hesitated, a glint of a tear coming to her eye. "I was giving my ignorant father one more chance to redeem himself. To let go of his outdated ideas and accept me as the daughter I actually was—not some prissy doll he could buy things for. If it had been up to him, neither me or my brother would have ever moved on with our lives. He would have kept us dependent on him. It may have worked on my brother, but I was done. I had to kill him and make sure someone else took the fall."

"Is that why you verbally attacked me at the *Koffee Hous*? Trying a little too desperately to point the finger after your original plan fell through?"

"I'm not desperate," she barked, her eyes bulging like a wild animal hunting its prey. "Besides, I *knew* you were spying on me, following me, trying to turn me in."

"What possible reason could I have for spying on you?"

Abigail smirked. "I saw how buddy, buddy you were with the cop. You're secretly working for him."

"Detective Mannor?"

"That's the one, all right."

Bert sighed. This girl really was a few screws loose. Bert had thought she was a little ditzy at first, but it seemed that she was an all-out psychopath.

"I wouldn't really call the detective and I friends."

"Don't lie to me. When you showed him that balloon, he took it into evidence. I knew you were onto me."

Bert's jaw dropped. "If you saw me pick up the balloon, that means you've been spying on *me*, not the other way around." Bert began to piece things together. "And you spied on your brother and your mom too, turned them into the police."

She shrugged. "Why not? If I can cause a little confusion, it's all the better for me." She giggled wickedly.

"You were trying to point the finger at someone to take the fall for the murder."

Narrowing her aim on Bert's chest, she smiled. "I guess it'll just have to be two murders, both with my brother's rifle."

"You don't have to do this."

"Say goodnight," she giggled.

Bert squeezed her eyes shut, knowing there was no way out this time, and waited for the pain to hit her.

"Don't even think about it," a man's voice demanded.

Opening her eyes again, Bert let out a sigh of relief upon seeing Detective Mannor stepping through the doorway.

"T-This isn't what it looks like," Abigail sputtered, putting up her hands. "I caught her trying to hide the evidence and took it away from her. See?" She held up the gun.

"Nice try. I'm sure once we test fingerprints on that weapon, we won't find a single one from Mrs. Hannah here, but I'm guessing there will be a few of yours." He motioned with his gun for her to drop her weapon. "Slowly set it down."

There was a tense moment of hesitation, and then Abigail began to weep as she set the rifle on the ground.

CAROLYN Q. HUNTER

Chapter 17

"How did you know where to find me?" Bert asked Detective Mannor the next morning. The previous night had been a blur of events, all ending with the detective arresting Abigail Blinkerton for the murder of her father Daniel Blinkerton.

He'd told Bert to head home and get some rest after what she'd been through. He even asked if she needed the paramedics.

Bert had, of course, declined this kind offer.

"Honestly, I didn't know you'd be up there. It was only after I got the autopsy report, which helped to determine which angle the bullet entered the body, that I got to even thinking about the possibility of it being a sniper." He waited a moment, trying to decide if he should admit the next sentence. "Of course, that balloon of yours helped a little, too."

"It did?" she exclaimed, a smile spreading across her lips.

The grimace on his face was an indication that he instantly regretted saying anything. Sighing, he gave in. "Yes. The rubber was burnt along the edges, indicating a bullet could have passed through."

"Wow. So, I was on the right track from the beginning."

"There were other things that seemed a little off, as well, that led me to guess it was Abigail. Soria Blinkerton shared the bit of information about her daughter. She'd realized her daughter was sneaking out to go shooting in the middle of the night a few years back and found boxes and boxes of books on guns hidden away in her bedroom. She started to get scared of the girl's behavior."

"She was acting strange, even back then?"

"According to her mother, she was mentally unstable and volatile."

Bert's jaw dropped. "So, *that's* probably the real reason Soria left. She was scared."

"The point is, we have Abigail in custody now and she won't be hurting anyone anymore. She'll probably plead insanity and be sent off to an institution. You won't have to worry about her coming after you." He puffed out his chest at this final comment like a male peacock strutting his stuff.

Bert let out another sigh of relief just thinking about the night before. "Well, thank heaven you figured it out when you did. Otherwise I'd be in the morgue, too."

"Well, that didn't happen. Let's keep it that way." He gave a firm nod. He stood up from the table. "I just stopped by to let you know. You won't have to be afraid of her coming after you again."

"I think I at least owe you a pie," she announced, moving back behind the display case. "More like a hundred pies, really," she laughed.

"That's quite all right."

"After all, you saved my life," Bert said.

"Mrs. Hannah, that isn't necessary." He put up both hands indicating he didn't need any handouts or favors.

"I insist, seriously." She opened the case and picked up a plate with a fresh slice of the popular chocolate-almond tart.

Mannor licked his lips, trying to decide if it was worth it to fight her on this.

"Come on. Sit down back down." She set the plate on a nearby table and pulled out a chair.

He grumbled wearily. "Oh, don't go begging. I'll eat it," he gave in, trying to hide his eagerness.

"Do you want a cup of coffee with it? I don't have pumpkin spice, but I think you'll still like it."

Pursing his lips, he agreed. "Sure. That might be nice."

Finally, his rugged exterior was beginning to melt. Bert rushed into the kitchen and grabbed a cup and set it in front of him. He'd begun to eat the pie, and she could see he was smiling. "You like it?"

"Mrs. Hannah, I hate to admit it, but this just might be the tastiest thing I ever had."

"I thought so," she smirked proudly. "Seriously, any time you're craving a pie, I'll give you a slice on the house. It's the least I can do."

Detective Mannor tried desperately to hide his glee at this offer, but Bert saw right through him. When it came to dessert, she could always read people.

"I think I could get used to that," he replied, raising his fork and taking another bite.

Bert hoped this was beginning of a friendship.

54352860R00100

Made in the USA
San Bernardino, CA
14 October 2017